082803

Ba Ba Sheep
Wouldn't Go to Sleep

A LUCAS • EVANS BOOK

13.99

Orchard Books
387 Park Avenue South
New York, New York 10016

Orchard Books Canada
20 Torbay Road
Markham, Ontario 23P 1G6

Orchard Books is a division of Franklin Watts, Inc.

Manufactured in the United States of America
Book design by Jean Krulis

10 9 8 7 6 5 4 3 2 1

The text of this book is set in ITC Bookman Light

89-B10212

Library of Congress Cataloging-in-Publication Data

Panek, Dennis. Ba Ba Sheep wouldn't go to sleep.

Summary: Ba Ba Sheep decides it would be fun to
stay up all night and play but he is so tired the next day
that he looks forward to going to bed.

[1. Sheep—Fiction. 2. Bedtime—Fiction. 3. Sleep—Fiction] I. Title.
PZ7.P1887Bab 1988   [E]   88-60090
ISBN 0-531-05776-3   ISBN 0-531-08376-4 (lib. bdg.)

Ba Ba Sheep
Wouldn't Go to Sleep

DENNIS PANEK

ORCHARD BOOKS
A division of Franklin Watts, Inc.
New York and London

Ba Ba Sheep didn't like to go to sleep.

"I'm not tired," he said. "I think I'll stay up."

No one heard him, so no one said "No!"

He got right out of bed and built a big town

and a long, long bridge with his wooden blocks.

Then he drove his trucks across the bridge
and sailed his boats under the bridge.

He flew his airplane over the town

until the dinosaurs attacked.

Just when he thought he might lie down for a minute, Ma Ma came into his room.

Ba Ba slowly got dressed. Very slowly.

Then he went downstairs.

"Are you all right?" asked Ma Ma.

"You look very sleepy."

She put a thermometer in Ba Ba's mouth
to be sure he didn't have a fever.

Ma Ma kissed him goodbye.

The school bus was waiting.

In math class he didn't hear the question.

At lunch time he wasn't very hungry.

At recess he quietly played on the swings.

Storytime was Ba Ba's favorite part of school.

At three o'clock, Mrs. Lamb

had to remind him to go home.

"Get some sleep, Ba Ba," said Mrs. Lamb.

"I'm not tired," said Ba Ba.

That night he ate only his applesauce.

"I don't feel like chewing," he said.

"Ba Ba, did you have a hard day?" asked Pa Pa.

"You look sleepy."

"I had a *long* day," said Ba Ba.

"May I be excused?"

Ba Ba climbed the stairs, put his pajamas
on, and brushed his teeth.

Ba Ba's sheets felt so smooth. The pillow was so soft.

The blanket was so warm. "Ah-h-h," said Ba Ba.

Ma Ma and Pa Pa looked in his door.

Ba Ba Sheep was sound asleep.

Goodnight, Ba Ba.